The Fisherman's Wife

A Sex Farce
With Sea Creatures

Steve Yockey

FOR PRODUCTION ENQUIRIES

UNITED STATES AND CANADA
Info@SamuelFrench.com
1-866-598-8449

UNITED KINGDOM AND EUROPE
Plays@SamuelFrench-London.co.uk
020-7255-4302

Each title is subject to availability from Samuel French, depending upon country of performance. Please be aware that *THE FISHERMAN'S WIFE* may not be licensed by Samuel French in your territory. Professional and amateur producers should contact the nearest Samuel French office or licensing partner to verify availability.

THE FISHERMAN'S WIFE was originally written for Impact Theatre. It opened as a rolling world premier on October 25, 2012 at LaVal's Subterranean Theatre in Berkeley, CA. the play was produced by Impact Theatre with Artistic Director, Melissa Hillman and Managing Director, Cheshire Isaacs. The Director was Ben Randle. Scenic design was by Anne Kendall, with lighting by Read Tuddenham and sound by Colin Trevor. Property design was by Tunuviel Luv, with costumes by Elizabeth Weston. The Stage Manager was Diana Strachan. The cast was as follows:

COOPER MINNOW. . . . . Maro Guevara

VANESSA MINNOW. . . . . Eliza Leoni

THOMAS BELL. . . . . Andrian J Anchondo

SQUID. . . . . Sarah Coykendall

OCTOPUS. . . . . Roy Landaverde

THE FISHERMAN'S WIFE opened as a rolling world premier on October 25, 2012 in the Speakeasy at Atwater Village Theatre in Los Angeles, CA. Produced by Ensemble Studio Theatre L.A. with Artistic Director Gates McFadden and Managing Director Michael Ruff, and with Producer Andrew Carlberg. The Director was Gates McFadden, and the Assistant Director was Oren Peleg. Lighting design was by Derrick McDaniel, with sound by Joseph Slawinski and costumes by Joe Kennedy. Puppet design and build was by John Burton. The Stage Manager was Priscilla Miranda. The cast was as follows:

COOPER MINNOW. . . . . Michael Hanson

VANESSA MINNOW. . . . . Sara McCarron

THOMAS BELL. . . . . Patrick Flanagan

SQUID. . . . . Kim Chueh

OCTOPUS. . . . . Gary Patent

PUPPETRY. . . . . Kevin Comartin, Kevin Riggin

CHARACTERS

COOPER MINNOW – A man, a young husband, a fisherman, doing his best to satisfy his wife's needs, frustrated and pent up; he grew up near the water

VANESSA MINNOW – A woman, a young wife, dissatisfied in her marriage that's not what she expected, frustrated and pent up; she often longs for more

THOMAS BELL – A man, a door-to-door salesman, the kind of person who has seen a lot of things and often has just what you need on hand - for the right price

SQUID – A "woman," very attractive, lithe, a manifestation of a tentacled sea creature, nurturing and seductive, but also bossy; kind of a sexual deviant

OCTOPUS – A "man," very attractive, sexy, a manifestation of a tentacled sea creature, an older brother, sassy and sarcastic; kind of a sexual deviant

NOTES

[ ] indicate overlapping dialogue

In a perfect world, Thomas Bell's tattoo puppet show will involve nautically themed marionettes and rod puppets with full-on detail and effects. But anything that reads "fantastic" and involves puppets will work.

Tentacled creatures appeared in Japanese erotica long before animated pornography. Among the most famous of the early instances is an illustration from the novel "Kinoe no komatsu" of 1814 by Katsushika Hokusai - an example of Japanese erotic art. A scholarly paper by Danielle Talerico showed that although western audiences have often interpreted Hokusai's design as rape, Japanese audiences of the Edo period would have associated it with consensual sex. Edo audiences would recognize the legend of the female abalone diver Tamatori who steals a jewel from the Dragon King. During her egress, the Dragon King and his sea-life minions pursue her. Furthermore, within the dialogue in the illustration itself, the diver and two octopuses express mutual enjoyment.

ACT ONE

(Lights rise on a bare stage except for a single chair. There might be a wood floor or the idea of a wood floor, but the space is otherwise bare. The back wall of the space is entirely covered by a hand painted mural that uses simple pictorial images, perhaps abstracted or crude, to depict all of the events that will eventually unfold in the play.)

(To one side, a small puppet theater quietly waits. A large, old-fashioned radio microphone on a tall stand sits next to the theater.)

*(**VANESSA** enters with a cup of coffee and a stack of magazines. She drops the stack with a thud and sits down in the chair. With a sigh, she picks up one the magazines and flips through it. **COOPER** enters in a rain slicker and carrying a fishing pole and a net. He waits. Maybe he taps his foot. She doesn't look up from the magazine.)*

COOPER. Im going out now.

VANESSA. Mm hm.

COOPER. In the boat.

VANESSA. Obviously.

COOPER. Yes. Well, yes. The radio says there might be a storm, but it doesn't look too bad yet.

VANESSA. All right.

COOPER. It might be a good time to actually make a substantial catch, really bring in a big haul.

VANESSA. In your big net.

COOPER. Yes. Because most of the other boats won't be out.

VANESSA. Mm hm.

COOPER. Are you listening?

VANESSA. Mm hm.

COOPER. Vanessa, I feel like we've been distant lately.

VANESSA. Have fun on the boat.

COOPER. I said I feel like there's this distance between us. Lately.

VANESSA. I suppose whatever kind of ice cream you want.

COOPER. Ice cream?

VANESSA. Oh, Cooper, you're still here?

COOPER. I know you do that on purpose.

VANESSA. Do you now.

COOPER. Look, since I have your full attention for an instant, the briefest of instants, I just wanted to say to you, okay, if something happens to me, because they're predicting a storm and all, if anything ever happens to me out on the water and I can't get back to shore, I just don't want you to grieve.

VANESSA. Oh.

COOPER. I want you to promise me that you'll find a new husband, a man who can, if possible, actually make you happy.

VANESSA. Absolutely.

COOPER. Oh. Good.

VANESSA. How long should I wait?

COOPER. I don't, what?

VANESSA. How long should I wait if you don't come back?

COOPER. How long should you wait if I'm lost at sea?

VANESSA. Yep.

COOPER. If I'm killed?

VANESSA. Just ballpark it for me.

COOPER. I hadn't really thought it through to that extent.

VANESSA. Ah.

COOPER. It was more of a gesture.

VANESSA. An empty gesture.

COOPER. No, now, I just hadn't thought it all the [way through.]

VANESSA. [Well, don't] worry about me. I won't be playing the pining widow.

COOPER. The "pining widow?"

VANESSA. Not my thing.

COOPER. No, of course not.

VANESSA. It's not even in my repertoire.

COOPER. Clearly. Huh, what was I thinking?

VANESSA. I honestly have no idea. Because nothing's going to happen to you, Cooper. It would be exciting if something did happen, but nothing ever happens so it won't. And here you are trying to make this big, random speech [before you...]

COOPER. [It's important to] discuss [these things.]

VANESSA. [Before you go] out on the boat into weather that's clearly not "going out on the boat into weather" weather. But don't worry, nothing ever happens ever. And we'll just go on. Like this.

COOPER. Sometimes things happen.

VANESSA. Never.

COOPER. We went to that restaurant in town last week.

VANESSA. Fuck that little shanty shack of a restaurant.

COOPER. Excuse me it was a nice evening.

VANESSA. It was like bathing in jellyfish, only less exciting.

COOPER. And you had the stuffed crab.

VANESSA. I had the less exciting snapper.

COOPER. I'm retty sure you had the [stuffed crab.]

VANESSA. [Oh my god,] Cooper, I had the snapper, the same snapper that was served at our wedding. And just like our wedding, the snapper was under cooked. Everything's under cooked. My whole fucking life is under cooked. I'm sorry if you don't think that's fair but I'm also not really sorry because I didn't choose this, I was bamboozled by the man I thought you were.

Now, just, go and catch fish and then come back so we can eat whatever I laughably try to make for dinner on that stove, which might only be frozen edamame because that's all we have right now, frozen edamame and a lot of sea salt to suck the moisture right out of our tongues, and then we can have some of the sandpaper on driftwood that passes for sex in our rock hard bed before passing out, bringing an end to another fucking monotonous day, and escaping into the arms of merciful sleep.

(pause)

COOPER. I enjoy our sex life.

VANESSA. No, you don't.

COOPER. Okay, I don't.

VANESSA. Honestly, how could you? It's basically imaginary at this point.

COOPER. This was a poorly timed conversation, I suppose. And I'm not prepared to, just, can we talk about it [after I get back?]

VANESSA. [It's supposed to] be more than this.

COOPER. Who told you that?

VANESSA. Everyone. Everyone! We're married!! We were so in love, Cooper, we were ridiculous and happy and I had so many dreams about sharing a life with my husband and none of them involved a house with no furniture that's about to fall into the sea.

COOPER. You picked out this house.

VANESSA. No. No, I said, "It looks fine." Which is not the same thing, you can hear when I say it that its not the same thing, can't you? "It looks fine." "It looks fine." Can you hear it? "It looks fine."

COOPER. Sadly, I can't read your mind. If I could, I'd have some idea of how to make you happy. Because believe me, this isn't how I envisioned married [life either.]

VANESSA. [Okay, all right,] look at this ring; do you see it? It's supposed to symbolize something beautiful to cherish, but instead it's like having some awful metallic leech permanently attached, sucking away, sucking the blood out of my entire body right through this one little finger.

COOPER. You're comparing our marriage [to a leech?]

VANESSA. [Suck, suck,] suck!

COOPER. A metallic leech?

VANESSA. Suck!!

COOPER. So wait, this is about our marriage or our sex life?

VANESSA. Yes!

COOPER. And the leech metaphor is [supposed to…]

VANESSA. [Oh god, it's] not your fault, it's not your fault; I'm just in a terrible mood. Forever.

COOPER. Fine.

VANESSA. Good. Because it's totally your fault.

COOPER. You just said that it [wasn't my…]

VANESSA. [I lied.]

COOPER. How is it my fault?

VANESSA. Just go fishing.

COOPER. Tell me right now how any of this [is my fault]

VANESSA. [Go fishing.]

COOPER. I demand that you explain how any [of this is…]

VANESSA. [Do you wanna go] back there and fuck me right now?

COOPER. Whoa! Where did [that come from?]

VANESSA. [Do. You. Want. To.] Go. Back. There. And. Fuck. Me?

COOPER. You don't think I will?!

VANESSA. No! No, I don't think you will. I wouldn't wield it like a weapon if I thought there was even a sliver of a chance that you'd actually do it. In fact, fuck going back there into that dimly lit cave of a bedroom, do it right here. Throw me on the floor and turn me inside out.

COOPER. Oh, that's attractive.

VANESSA. It doesn't have to be attractive, nobody's going to see it!

COOPER. It's not attractive to the ear.

VANESSA. Well, at least it'll feel good! Maybe. Or maybe it'll be fucking awful.

COOPER. Now, hold [on a minute.]

VANESSA. [Maybe it'll be like] having a bunch of fish hooks dragged across my skin, but it would be something. Come on, come on!

COOPER. I have to take the boat out.

VANESSA. Oh my god! Just to be super clear: you'd rather take the rickety old fishing boat out into a potentially lethal [storm and...]

COOPER. [I said bad, maybe] bad, [not lethal.]

VANESSA. [I want you to] fuck me!

COOPER. I don't want to!

VANESSA. And that's why it's your fault!

(*pause*)

COOPER. A relationship takes two people, Vanessa. I won't be [responsible...]

VANESSA. [You're really] eating into my time right now, time that I could be reading about other exciting people living exciting lives that aren't my life thus pushing me further into depression and I'd really like to get on with it because I'm really close to achieving the critical mass needed to give suicide a real go.

COOPER. Well, look, don't do that.

VANESSA. Ugh, I'm not going to do that.

(*He starts to leave but turns back.*)

COOPER. But if you do kill yourself then make sure you get it right because we don't have anything even close to the degree of health insurance to cover hospitalization if you try to take your own life and only maim yourself or end up hooked up to a machine by doing a mediocre job.

VANESSA. Don't you worry about my follow through.

COOPER. And I'm not really a caretaker.

VANESSA. Tell me about it.

COOPER. I don't really want to take care of you.

VANESSA. Got it.

COOPER. You specifically.

VANESSA. I said, "Got it."

COOPER. You know where I keep the revolver, right?

VANESSA. I do.

COOPER. It's on the shelf in the top of the bedroom [closet]

VANESSA. [I said,] "I do!"

COOPER. It's off to the side in the back corner of the shelf. It might be hard for you to find because it's hidden underneath that stack of adult magazines that you hate so much.

VANESSA. Yep!

COOPER. My well-worn stack of adult magazines [that you hate.]

VANESSA. [I said, "Yep!"]

COOPER. And you know that you should put it in your mouth, not hold it up to your temple, so you don't just blind yourself, right?

VANESSA. Are you fucking [kidding me?]

COOPER. [Because that's] not the "excitement" you're looking for; it's awful and it falls into the category of "needing care" from a caregiver and, again, that's not me. You understand, [right?]

VANESSA. [Now I do,] thanks!!

COOPER. Because you're not the only one who isn't [in the best mood.]

VANESSA. [You mentioned taking the] boat out [now, is that happening?!]

COOPER. [Oh, you were listening,] [because I couldn't tell!]

VANESSA. [Bring back fish unless] you just want edamame!

COOPER. You know I fucking hate edamame!

VANESSA. That's why I said, "Bring back fish!"

COOPER. Great! I'll see when I [get home later!]

VANESSA. [Be safe!]

COOPER. I will!

VANESSA. Love you!

> *(He storms out.* **VANESSA** *sinks back into the chair with a powerful exhale as* **THOMAS** *appears in a spot light with a carpetbag sitting next to him. He is sharply dressed in shirt, tie, and suspenders with high shine polished shoes. He is rolling up his sleeves to reveal strong arms covered in nautically themed tattoos. He also wears a pair of round spectacles that he periodically takes off, wipes with a handkerchief. He's a smooth operator.)*
>
> *(He pulls the old-fashioned microphone onto stage and a spotlight appears. He taps the microphone for sound and then clears his throat.)*

THOMAS. There are so many wonderful things about living in this seaside town: the cool, crisp air, the salty smell that keeps you a little more alert, the lush greenery climbing up from craggy rocks and gray sand, like unexpected plumes of determined life. And the mysteries of the dark water as it churns away full of creatures and secrets. It can really be inspiring if you stop and look. And of course, there's a lifestyle, a kind of "fisherman's" lifestyle. Rough hands, hard work, all that. It has a certain appeal to some people. So those are some of the best things. One of the worst things about living in this little seaside town is the amazing difficulty you can run into when trying to procure anything that might be a bit out of the ordinary. Trying to get your hands on anything that might not be on the shelf at the general store, you know? Luckily, you don't have to worry too much about that because someone like me is always making the rounds. And

I'm happy to deliver anything I can get my hands on. I'm happy to do anything I can to help.

(He sets the microphone aside again as the spotlight fades. He makes sure the cord is out of the way and then knocks in the air as if on a door. He stamps his foot to add the Foley sound. **VANESSA** *looks up, startled by the knocking.)*

VANESSA. Who is it?

THOMAS. Salesman.

VANESSA. No, thank you. Go away.

THOMAS. Travelling salesman.

VANESSA. I said, "No, thank you. Go away."

*(***THOMAS*** loosens his tie and unbuttons a few buttons, revealing more tattoo work.)*

THOMAS. Alt-attractive travelling salesman.

VANESSA. Oh?

THOMAS. Attractive in an alternative way, you understand.

VANESSA. Well then.

(She gets up and heads for the door. She stops, heads back and straightens up the magazine pile. She examines this. She shakes her head, quickly walks off and returns with some kind of large wooden block. She places the magazines on the wooden block and examines this.)

THOMAS. Also charming. A charming and alt-attractive travelling salesman.

VANESSA. I'm coming, just a moment.

(She quickly adjusts the chair and then turns to welcome **THOMAS** *into her home.)*

THOMAS. Ah. Good morning, mam.

VANESSA. Vanessa. Vanessa Minnows. Not mam, please.

THOMAS. Of course. And I'm Thomas Bell.

VANESSA. You are very alternatively attractive, Thomas.

THOMAS. Isn't that the truth?

VANESSA. It really is.

THOMAS. You look lovely this morning, such a healthy flush in your cheek.

VANESSA. I was yelling at my husband.

THOMAS. Oh no, I hate that for you. Aren't men just the worst sometimes? Well, some men. Not all men. Not me, for instance. I hope you don't mind if I set my bag down?

VANESSA. Not at all. Let me just clear this off.

(She grabs the stack of magazines from the wooden block, walks to the edge of the stage and throws them from view.)

There.

THOMAS. Thank you.

(He sets his bag down on the wooden block and opens it. He pulls his tie off and maybe unbuttons a few more buttons.)

Now, oh, have a seat please.

(She sits in the chair. Then immediately starts to get up again.)

VANESSA. Oh, do you need coffee or water or, I don't know, I think we have some gin.

THOMAS. Gin?

VANESSA. I know we have some gin.

THOMAS. I'm fine, please. Just sit back and I'll present my wares.

VANESSA. That sounds fun.

(She sits again.)

THOMAS. There are so many wonderful things about living in this seaside town: the cool, crisp air, the salty smell that keeps you a little more alert, the lush greenery climbing up from craggy rocks and gray sand, like [unexpected plumes…]

VANESSA. [This part is] boring.

THOMAS. I'm sorry?

VANESSA. This part is boring. Maybe if you took your shirt off? I don't know. But if you're trying to sell me on the natural beauty of this place, that's gonna be an uphill climb.

THOMAS. I'll just skip to the end of this part.

VANESSA. Great.

THOMAS. One of the worst things about living in this little seaside town is the [amazing…]

VANESSA. [This is] already much better.

THOMAS. Great. One of the worst things is the difficulty you can run into when trying to procure anything that might be a bit out of the ordinary. Luckily, you dont have to worry too much about that because I'm happy to deliver anything I can get my hands on. I'm happy to do anything I can to help. Is there anything in particular that you may need?

VANESSA. Thomas Bell, that's a big question.

THOMAS. I'll help if I can.

VANESSA. Are you sure I can't get you some gin?

THOMAS. You know, I shouldn't. But…if you're having some then I will, too.

VANESSA. This is going so well. Just a sec.

(She rushes off.)

THOMAS. This is quite a spare little home you have here. It's such an interesting design choice, very bold.

(She rushes back on with large tumblers full of straight gin. She hands one to him.)

VANESSA. It's not a choice; we don't have anything. I thought we would, but we don't. Maybe we will some day, but it's looking pretty bleak. My husband comes from a huge fishing family, all very successful. He's not, though. He's not. Oh, but it's very nice of you to try to put a positive spin on it.

THOMAS. You're very up front, arcn't you?

(She drinks her entire glass of gin in one long chug and throws the glass offstage.)

VANESSA. I hate this place. Are you going to drink that?

*(**THOMAS** begins to sip his gin. Clearly it's straight. And strong.)*

Look, you're alternatively attractive and someone that "looks" sexually active, at least in my estimation, is that right?

THOMAS. Yes.

VANESSA. I can't help noticing your shirt is still on.

THOMAS. For now.

VANESSA. Oh. Well. Let me ask you, what is it do you think that would cause a young husband, a disappointing non-man of a husband, a poor excuse for a fisherman and terrible provider husband, to suddenly recoil at the idea of even touching his wife?

THOMAS. Ah.

VANESSA. I mean, it's not like the sex was ever good, but it was sometimes satisfying. He has the size, the girth you know, to be sometimes satisfying in spite of his really tragically poor technique.

THOMAS. Well, that's good.

VANESSA. Oh now, I don't know about "good." He needs training, not training, instruction, but he's so defensive about everything.

THOMAS. It's a sensitive topic for some men.

VANESSA. I guess I always assumed that if a young man didn't learn sex on his own at some point, through, just, happenstance, that eventually some other observant man in his life would take pity on him and take him to a prostitute, or a "generous woman" I guess, like an archaic small town tradition. Is that a small town tradition?

THOMAS. I'm not from a small town.

VANESSA. Me either. It's so frustrating. But clearly no one ever did that for my husband and now he's just awful, no, no, he's not anything because he won't touch me and I'm climbing out of my fucking skin, do you have anything for that?

(Thomas glances down at his bag.)

THOMAS. As a matter of fact, I have any number of things that might put the spark back in the bedroom. So to speak. Let me see here…

(He reaches into his bag but comes up empty handed. He's changed his mind.)

You know, to find just the right thing, let me ask you a few questions. You don't mind, do you? All strictly confidential.

VANESSA. I want something to reinvigorate our sex life.

THOMAS. So what I'm hearing from you is that you're in need of a product that will inspire some [kind of…]

VANESSA. [I want] something to reinvigorate our sex life.

THOMAS. Is there a particular avenue of device or aid [that you're…]

VANESSA. [I want] something to reinvigorate our sex life!

THOMAS. Got it.

VANESSA. Thank goodness.

(He reaches into the bag. Far into the bag. Impossibly far, probably up to his shoulder. He pulls out an ornate hatchet.)

THOMAS. Not that; ignore that.

(He pulls out a wooden baby doll.)

Definitely not that.

VANESSA. That's adorable.

THOMAS. It's really not. If you knew what it was used for.

VANESSA. What's it used for?

(He reaches in again, pulling out a series of woodcuts in a stack. He blows dust off and looks them over.)

THOMAS. Oh no, not these either. These are patently for a more adventurous couple.

VANESSA. I want to be adventurous, what is it?

THOMAS. No, no. You wouldn't like these.

(He sets the woodcut prints down away from her.)

VANESSA. Is everything in that impossibly deep bag "not for me." Jesus Christ, I want to see them. Now.

THOMAS. If you insist, I suppose.

(He hands her the woodcuts. As she examines them, her face registers horror and fascination.)

VANESSA. These are patently for a more adventurous couple.

THOMAS. They are examples of historical shokushu goukan.

VANESSA. "Shokushu goukan." How exotic.

THOMAS. It's roughly translated as "tentacle erotica."

VANESSA. It's very graphic.

THOMAS. Or "tentacle rape."

VANESSA. Oh. Now it's even more graphic. But… I don't know. She certainly seems to be enjoying her time with those enthusiastic sea creatures.

THOMAS. I suppose that's one way to look at. You know these are early examples, but they've inspired an entire genre of erotica. Sadly, now it mostly involves young girls and well-endowed monsters, but it started from a place of genuine love for the sea.

(VANESSA turns the woodcuts at different angles. It's evident that none of the angles make them more appealing.)

VANESSA. Hmmm.

THOMAS. I really didn't think you'd enjoy these. Most people don't.

VANESSA. Like most people, I don't. It's absolutely disgusting.

THOMAS. I can put them away.

VANESSA. Hold on, I'm just noticing that behind the sea creatures penetrating this woman in multiple orifices, there's a dock that looks just like the dock where my husband moors his boat.

THOMAS. Not really.

VANESSA. Exactly like the dock where my husband moors his boat.

THOMAS. Such a coincidence.

VANESSA. In fact, that looks like his boat.

(**THOMAS** *quickly pulls the woodcuts away and reaches back into the bag.*)

THOMAS. I can almost guarantee the authenticity and age of these woodcuts, especially for the price. So it wouldn't and couldn't be his boat unless they were fakes. I do hope that's not what you're suggesting? Suggesting that I just sat down next to the dock when I first arrived in this town and carved them myself using the fine edge of that hatchet from my bag, which I absolutely did not do.

VANESSA. I wasn't suggesting that at all.

THOMAS. Good. Now, let's see what else I have.

VANESSA. But I was suggesting that I'm almost certain that the dock in that woodcut is the same dock where my husband moors his boat.

THOMAS. Look, it's a really universal woodcut, okay?

VANESSA. In any event, I'm not sure I understand who exactly would find those pictures sexually exciting.

THOMAS. To each his own. Ah!

(*He pulls out an enormous wooden phallus. It's probably a phallus. It's ambiguous enough that it could potentially just be decorative art.*)

VANESSA. Oh my!

THOMAS. This might just do the trick. It's said to have properties that greatly increase sex drive.

VANESSA. It's intimidating.

THOMAS. Is that right?

VANESSA. I mentioned that my husband, while terrible in almost all respects, is very well equipped. But there are limits.

THOMAS. Well it isn't meant for practical use. Let me be very clear. I'd hate for you to injure yourself by being too ambitious. You simply keep it near the bed and it's said to infuse your activities with a higher level of intensity. And you could perhaps also rest a hat on it.

VANESSA. How practical.

THOMAS. A summer hat or a fascinator, a pill box hat, any hat really.

VANESSA. Hats. Got it.

*(As **THOMAS** drifts into this reverie, he holds the wooden phallus with both hands at waist level. Intentional or not, this creates a suggestive pose that definitely catches **VANESSA**'s attention.)*

THOMAS. You see my father was a haberdasher, so I do tend to get nostalgic on the topic. He owned a little haberdashery near the sea where you could get all kinds of buttons, ribbons, zippers, any little notions for sewing, but he also had a lovely array of women's hats.

VANESSA. At the haberdashery.

THOMAS. Near the sea.

VANESSA. Is any of this memory lane business filling you with the desire to take off our shirt?

*(**THOMAS** let's the phallus fall to his side.)*

THOMAS. No.

VANESSA. How unfortunate. Well then let's not talk about hats anymore, I find them to be silly. Let's focus again on this statue?

THOMAS. Totem.

VANESSA. What kind of guarantee does it come with?

THOMAS. Oh, now, you can trust me. We just met, but I have a trustworthy look, don't I? And frankly, I don't really peddle in warrantees and the such. Not with this kind of product. It would be almost impossible [to offer…]

VANESSA. [Well then I'm] going to have to insist on a trial run.

THOMAS. Im amenable to that idea.

VANESSA. Exceptional.

THOMAS. When will your husband be back?

(She throws her arms around **THOMAS** *and begins kissing him passionately. He stands for a moment then returns the kiss. She finishes unbuttoning his shirt and strips it off revealing his chest, back, and arms covered in nautical tattoos. She reaches aggressively into his pants and squeezes. He winces. She grabs the phallus with her free hand and leads him to the bedroom.)*

*(***OCTOPUS** *and* **SQUID** *make their way on. They are both wearing form-fitting 1940s style swimwear in shades of blue or brown.* **OCTOPUS** *is carrying a barrel. He sets it down and perches on it as* **SQUID** *leans against a wall playing with a seashell.)*

OCTOPUS. So he's so big and he has this really thick baleen.

SQUID. So like, in his mouth? That's the kinda' white stuff that strains the little fish, right?

OCTOPUS. Yes.

SQUID. So can I just, I don't understand why you need the barrel.

OCTOPUS. I don't need it; I like it. It has character. And it was just floating there. So no one's going to miss it.

SQUID. So it's just more junk to shove under our dock.

*(***OCTOPUS** *dry humps the barrel.)*

OCTOPUS. The wood feels good against my skin.

SQUID. You're going to just rub on it inappropriately, aren't you?

OCTOPUS. If I want to I will. So think of it as furnishing, that's how I think of it. And I was in the middle of a story.

SQUID. So go on then.

OCTOPUS. So like I said, he's basically this massive whale.

SQUID. Size queen.

OCTOPUS. And so he wants me to rub his baleen. Like this…

(He mimes what looks like the universally recognized physicality for manual sex.)

SQUID. Ha! Nice. So I had this sailor once who could only cum if I was rubbing his teeth, making that awful squeaking noise.

OCTOPUS. I hate that noise.

SQUID. Right? So did you do what the whale wanted?

OCTOPUS. So I mean, I couldn't say no.

SQUID. You're such a slut.

OCTOPUS. I know, right?

*(They both laugh. **COOPER** walks in. They stop and stare at him.)*

COOPER. Excuse me.

OCTOPUS & SQUID. What?

COOPER. My boat is moored just here at the dock and I can't seem to get the anchor up. The chain seems to have been pulled up under here.

OCTOPUS & SQUID. So?

COOPER. I didn't mean to interrupt.

OCTOPUS & SQUID. So what, you want your anchor back?

COOPER. Do you have it?

OCTOPUS & SQUID. Maybe.

COOPER. I don't mean to be rude, but do you always speak in unison?

OCTOPUS & SQUID. Not always.

COOPER. Oh. Good. It's a little unnerving.

OCTOPUS & SQUID. So…?

COOPER. And it's a little cold out for that kind of swimwear, isn't it?

OCTOPUS. Swimwear?

COOPER. Those, I guess, sexy swimsuits?

SQUID. Oh, so he totally sees swimwear. He sees "people" wearing swimwear. When he looks at us.

OCTOPUS. When he looks at us?

SQUID. So it's one of those magical sea creature things, just go with it.

OCTOPUS. Fun. I so love being from the sea.

SQUID. Right?

COOPER. Yes, well, anyway there's a storm coming, according to the weather reports, and I'd like to get some fishing done before it gets bad.

OCTOPUS. Weather reports are stupid.

COOPER. Be that as it may, I'm [going to…]

SQUID. [So then] we'll give you your anchor back.

OCTOPUS. We will?

SQUID. Yes.

OCTOPUS. Why?

SQUID. But first you have to give us something.

OCTOPUS. Ohhhh, I get it.

COOPER. Well, it's technically my anchor. I'm not really prepared to barter with you for something that's already mine. I do that enough with my wife. Oh! Don't tell her I said that. I suppose if push comes to shove I can just go get the local constable and report you for theft.

(They laugh at him.)

Listen, it's been a rough morning. Just give me back my anchor.

OCTOPUS. So it's tit.

SQUID. For tat.

OCTOPUS. And this.

SQUID. For that.

OCTOPUS. So, just to be clear, the "this" in that little mantra is your anchor. And the "that" is what we want. You see?

COOPER. What exactly is it that you want?

SQUID. I think I want a kiss.

COOPER. Oh, I'm sorry. I'm a married man.

OCTOPUS. So you're a happily married man?

COOPER. I'm not sure that's a fair or relevant distinction with two oddly inquisitive strangers under a dock.

OCTOPUS. So, right, that's what I thought. How hung are you?

COOPER. What?

OCTOPUS. Oh, so I asked, "How hung are you?"

COOPER. Uhhhh, I heard you.

OCTOPUS. So then why did you say, "What?" Oh! I offended you; I offended him by asking about his manhood.

SQUID. He's so interested in those kinds of things.

OCTOPUS. I so am.

SQUID. Maybe too interested.

OCTOPUS. Don't start.

COOPER. Look, I just want my anchor back.

SQUID. So I'm still feeling this out, and tell me if I'm wrong, but I'm guessing that I appear to you as a very attractive woman?

OCTOPUS. In swimwear.

SQUID. Yes, an attractive woman in "sexy" swimwear.

COOPER. Dated swimwear, or retro, whatever they're calling it. But yes, that's obviously true. Although not very humble.

(**OCTOPUS** *laughs*).

SQUID. Well, theres no accounting for taste. And you look like a man that can really kiss when given the chance to cut free and just do it. I can really tell, you know? I'm experienced.

OCTOPUS. She's so experienced.

SQUID. Shut-up.

OCTOPUS. I mean just so crazy experienced.

SQUID. Anyway, I can just tell. About the kissing. It's in the lips, the way they move. Mmmm. The way they bend when someone makes words, someone like you. When someone like you "wets" them. You can see if there's strength and I see all kinds of strength in your lips. Tasty, yummy strength.

COOPER. You're mistaken.

SQUID. So go ahead and prove me wrong?

COOPER. I'm perfectly certain that my wife would not like that at all.

OCTOPUS. So I'm getting from your tone of voice that your wife doesn't really like anything.

SQUID. Mmm, I'm getting that, too.

(**SQUID** *reaches out and pulls* **COOPER** *by the hand over to her.*)

COOPER. She's just…she's just really unhappy.

OCTOPUS & SQUID. That's hard.

COOPER. And I'm trying to be a good fisherman, I really am. But it feels like everything I try falls short for her.

OCTOPUS & SQUID. So hard.

COOPER. And the more I disappoint her, the more I'm afraid of disappointing her and the harder it is to even muster up the will to try to make her happy.

OCTOPUS & SQUID. So hard.

COOPER. Im sorry to whine to you about it.

OCTOPUS & SQUID. Not a problem.

COOPER. I just don't have anyone else to talk to about anything.

OCTOPUS & SQUID. We so get it.

COOPER. You guys aren't the anchor-thieving hooligans that I initially thought you were at all.

SQUID. That's sweet. And just think: you were a very successful fisherman today.

OCTOPUS. So Successful.

SQUID. Right? You caught yourself a really nice squid.

COOPER. I did?

OCTOPUS. And an octopus.

COOPER. But I didn't even go out on the boat.

OCTOPUS. Me. I'm the octopus. She's the squid.

COOPER. I don't understand.

OCTOPUS. Its a magical sea creature thing; you can't be that dense.

SQUID. Aww, he just doesn't get it yet.

(She kisses him gently.)

COOPER. That…that wasn't bad at all.

*(She smiles. Suddenly **OCTOPUS** wraps his arm around **COOPER**'s neck, violently putting him into a chokehold. **SQUID** puts her hand to his lips and shoves it into his mouth causing his body to go rigid. She reaches her other hand into the front of **COOPER**'s pants as **OCTOPUS** slips his free hand into the back of **COOPER**'s pants. **COOPER** mumbles something unintelligible, muted by **SQUID**'s hand. Their mouths are all over him as they drag him out of sight.)*

*(Suddenly **VANESSA** enters wrapped in a sheet. She crashes down into the chair, drinking a gigantic glass of water, props her feet up on the wooden block, and wipes the hair out of her face. **THOMAS** follows. He is only wearing colorful, skimpy underwear and his tattooed upper body is completely visible. He is also drinking a huge glass of water.)*

THOMAS. Hydration is so important.

VANESSA. I will buy that statue.

THOMAS. Totem.

VANESSA. If that was any indication of how it works, then I will buy it.

THOMAS. Well, I don't usually have any complaints regarding my prowess, but let's say it was the totem and you can just write me a check.

VANESSA. How much is it?

THOMAS. Now Mrs. Minnow, stop and [ask yourself…]

VANESSA. [Ah ah ah,] it's Vanessa.

THOMAS. Now Vanessa, stop and ask yourself if you can you really put a price on that kind of performance?

VANESSA. Oh, you absolutely can. But if you want to wait to talk about money, that's fine. I'm still drinking this water. And my hips ache.

THOMAS. Sorry about that.

VANESSA. No, no, I'm just out of practice.

THOMAS. Are you quite sure your husband won't be home any moment?

VANESSA. He's on the boat.

THOMAS. Because that's usually how these things work, plot wise.

VANESSA. He's on the boat.

THOMAS. The husbands just walk right in.

VANESSA. I really don't know how I could be any clearer as to his current location on a boat out in the sea.

THOMAS. I'm overly cautious; I really do apologize. Only, I'd hate for him to find us like this. And all of the ensuing messiness.

VANESSA. I honestly don't even know what he'd do, Tom. I'd like to call you Tom, oh, that's fun, isn't it?

THOMAS. I prefer Thomas.

VANESSA. Ah, well, Thomas, I'd like to think he'd kill you. I don't wish for you to be dead, you understand. I'm not a sadist. But I do long for that kind of unbridled rage, driven by betrayal, driven by a near psychopathic jealousy.

THOMAS. Yikes.

VANESSA. Because it would ultimately come from some underlying passion. For me. And that passion, my alt-attractive fling, is sorely lacking.

THOMAS. But then I'd be dead.

VANESSA. Well, you completely missed the point of the hypothetical.

THOMAS. Well, I didn't care for it.

VANESSA. It's not that I don't love him. I do love him. That's probably hard to believe, but I do. I love him so much that I want to take a brick and lovingly smash his face in for not being the man I love so much.

THOMAS. That is very violent.

VANESSA. Well sometimes there's a place for violence.

THOMAS. I beg to differ.

VANESSA. Oh, do you?

THOMAS. Violence is never the answer.

VANESSA. Well, you're having sex on a regular basis so I don't care what you think about what I think about the place of violence in my marriage.

THOMAS. Marriage is difficult.

VANESSA. There's a fucking Earth-shattering revelation. Go tell it on the mountain, Thomas. Go preach it from door to door!

THOMAS. I'm noting the unwarranted sarcasm in your tone.

VANESSA. Our life here is just so mundane, day after day. I don't even know why I'm talking about it; I don't want to talk about him right now.

THOMAS. You seem to want to talk about him.

VANESSA. I just said I don't want to talk about him.

THOMAS. And yet, you continue to talk about him.

(*She starts to respond and then stops.*)

Mm hm.

VANESSA. Fine. Tell me something amazing about you then. Tell me about your tattoos.

THOMAS. Ah, you like them? Well, they all mean different things, I suppose. Each one has its own story, all from different times. In a way, they tell the story of my life here by the sea.

VANESSA. How about I pick one out and you tell me what it means?

THOMAS. Hmm, that seems very familiar. I…should really be on my way.

VANESSA. That was fast.

THOMAS. I'd stay if I could, obviously, but there are just so many houses and each one needs [my attention.]

VANESSA. [Oh my god,] please. It's not like I'm asking for intimacy. Try to still that knee jerk male reaction, no one's falling in love.

THOMAS. That seems like a huge generalization. Frankly, you seem prone to huge generalizations.

VANESSA. Maybe. I'm lonely sitting here all day; I don't have any hobbies. I tried knitting but it was a complete disaster that somehow ended up in the death of our cat, bizarrely, and Sudoku puzzles make me want to claw my flesh off a handful at a time, plus we never have any sharpened pencils; why the hell don't we ever have any sharpened pencils?! Now look, we fucked, a lot, which was so absolutely what I needed, you were quite deft at it, and now Im buying the statue.

THOMAS. Totem.

VANESSA. Whatever, I'm buying the mystical phallic hat rack thing. So just humor me with a few stories about your ink, Thomas Bell. All right?

(He relents, presenting himself to her.)

THOMAS. Where would you like to start?

VANESSA. Let me see, hmm… I think the big one on your arm.

THOMAS. The anchor?

VANESSA. Yes.

THOMAS. It's just an anchor.

VANESSA. Okay.

THOMAS. Well, it's representative of growing up around boats and blah, blah, blah. But it doesn't really have a specific story attached, per se.

VANESSA. How about the blue fish?

THOMAS. This fish?

VANESSA. Yes.

THOMAS. It's just a fish.

VANESSA. I'm starting to feel very mislead here; you've done a poor job of managing my expectations as an audience member.

THOMAS. Ah, but this other fish, the green fish? That one has quite a story.

(As **THOMAS** *starts to tell his story, the lights in the room dim a bit and gentle underscoring begins as petite foot lights in front of the small puppet theater rise. The events of* **THOMAS** *' story unfold on the little stage with puppets.* **VANESSA** *is delighted.)*

VANESSA. Ohhhh.

THOMAS. This was long ago, when I was still a novice traveling salesman. I didn't know yet the safest waterways or how to gauge the danger of situations as I moved from house to house and town to town.

(Little **THOMAS.** *with his little bag passes houses.)*

One day I happened to find myself on a small raft in the sea. Stranded due to a misunderstanding with a Captain's wife. All alone. Or so I thought.

(Little **THOMAS.** *is on a little raft in the water.)*

VANESSA. Oh my.

THOMAS. As I pondered my predicament, the water near me started to move and dance. Suddenly an immense fish, it must have been a fish of some kind although

I've never seen the like, began to rise from the water. It was monstrous with a gigantic mouth full of razor teeth, scales like jagged rocks and these long, graceful fins.

(*A little sea monster rises out of the water.*)

I stayed very still, but a single yellow eye landed on me and one of the fins reached out and encircled me, squeezing tight, lifting me up off the raft. I grabbed my bag, thank goodness it occurred to me.

VANESSA. Oh my!

(*The little sea monster picks up little* **THOMAS**.)

THOMAS. With me in its grip, the beast slowly rolled partially onto its side, exposing a much softer pink underbelly. As I struggled, the beast began to rub me against the softest, moistest parts of its exposed underbelly.

(*The little sea monster rolls over on its side and rubs little* **THOMAS** *back and forth over its lower belly.*)

The smell was awful. Rubbing me back and forth, faster and faster, rhythmically, dipping me in and out of the water. I thought it must be trying to drown me, so I desperately gasped for air. This went on for a while and the beast began to make noises, these deep, rumbling noises. Then, all at once, its entire body tensed as it released a deafening moan. I found myself suddenly covered with a thick, sticky substance rushing from the underbelly.

(*Fluid erupts from the lower underbelly of the little sea monster all over little* **THOMAS**. *It might even erupt out of the puppet theater. It is messy.*)

VANESSA. Um…whoa.

THOMAS. Just so thick and sticky.

VANESSA. I got it.

THOMAS. Unbelievably sticky.

VANESSA. I said, "I got it."

THOMAS. The beast became still then and loosened its grip just enough for me to reach into my bag and find my hatchet. It began to lift me up towards its mouth and I knew that would be the end of me. So I hacked and hacked away with my hatchet at its fin-like appendage until the beast cried out and finally released me.

(Little **THOMAS** *struggles and breaks free, falling into the water. The little sea monster disappears again.)*

I barely managed to avoid falling into its waiting mouth, all those teeth. As I splashed down into the sea, the beast slowly submerged into the dark water, nursing its wounds. I didn't know what to do, weak, out of breath, covered in thick, sticky beast juice, barely able to stay afloat. It seemed hopeless.

VANESSA. That does sound low.

THOMAS. But just then, a green fish appeared. It was a beautiful fish that almost seemed to glow in the waves.

(A little green fish appears).

At first I was afraid, but it became clear the fish was no threat. It gently began to lick and nibble at the sticky liquid the larger beast had left.

(Many little green fish appear, lifting **THOMAS** *up.)*

And then there were more green fish, hundreds, fighting in a frenzy to eat away the thick, sticky coat of liquid.

VANESSA. Sounds like an orgy of fish.

THOMAS. Does it?

VANESSA. You know, never mind. I didn't mean to interrupt.

THOMAS. So as all of the little green fish struggled to get to me, writhing on top of each other in this undulating mass, I was held afloat and gently carried by their bodies through the water until I could see land. I emerged from the sea cleansed and wiser for the experience.

(Little **THOMAS** *reaches land and stands on his own two feet.)*

VANESSA. You could have died?

THOMAS. Yes.

VANESSA. You could have died in the masticating jaws of a giant sea monster.

THOMAS. Well, a very large fish.

VANESSA. A fish with intense personal needs.

THOMAS. I'm sorry?

VANESSA. Well, the way you described it, all of the rubbing?

THOMAS. But the point is this: there are any number of things we can't understand about the world or our lives, but when we most need help, help will be provided.

VANESSA. Oh, wow, I couldn't disagree more.

THOMAS. And now I have this green fish to remind me.

VANESSA. Fascinating.

THOMAS. Isn't it?

VANESSA. I mean just incredibly naïve as to the way that the actual world works in terms of praying for magical rescue and blissfully ignorant as to the clear, sexually aggressive intent of that sea monster, but yes: absolutely fascinating.

*(***COOPER*** enters, naked and wrapped in a tarp of some kind. He looks stunned. More specifically, he looks like he was just violated in a myriad of ways by aggressive sea creatures. He probably walks a bit askew.)*

*(The puppet theater goes still, the lights abruptly restore and underscoring vanishes. ***THOMAS*** looks like he might run.)*

VANESSA. Cooper!

THOMAS. Your husband?

VANESSA. Back from the sea!

THOMAS. So! So! So as you can see, Mrs. Minnow, this particular pair of underwear would be an excellent purchase for your husband.

VANESSA. Yes! Yes!

THOMAS. And I was more than happy to model them for you.

VANESSA. Thank you!

THOMAS. As a part of my commitment to customer [service.]

(VANESSA is breathless and overwrought as she throws the back of her hand to her forehead and goes way over the top...)

VANESSA. [Oh, stop it,] Thomas! He's caught us, we've been found out. We've been discovered. Please, Cooper, please don't let your rage get the best of you as you savagely beat this travelling salesman or gut him like a fish and then passionately punish me for this sexual betrayal.

THOMAS. Gut me like a fish?

VANESSA. Cooper, please!

(COOPER shuffles into the room not really hearing any of this.)

THOMAS. I abhor violence in all forms, so [I beg you to...]

VANESSA. [Please! Don't!] Lose! Control!

(They wait. Tense. VANESSA is still way over the top, even in her hopeful suspense. COOPER shuffles a bit further into the room. The tension is broken as VANESSA and THOMAS exchange a glance and relax.)

THOMAS. Mr. Minnow?

VANESSA. Cooper, theres a man in his underwear and I'm sitting here barely covered in a bed sheet, a sweat-soaked, fluid-soiled bed sheet.

THOMAS. What you're doing now is, technically speaking, the opposite of getting away with this.

VANESSA. Shut-up! Cooper, everything about this tableau screams illicit sex, he has tattoos for God's sake! What the fuck is wrong with you?

THOMAS. He seems like perhaps he's in some kind of shock.

VANESSA. Shock?

THOMAS. Im no doctor, but that's how it appears.

VANESSA. He's not in shock. He's just an awful, disappointing excuse for…

(She is cut off as purple slime of some kind erupts from **COOPER**'s mouth and he falls on his knees and begins to cry. The kind of crying that involves no shame or self-control. **VANESSA** pulls her sheet up and rushes to hold him.)

THOMAS. Oh no!

VANESSA. What the [fuck?!]

THOMAS. [I think I have] something in my bag [that might…]

VANESSA. [Cooper! Cooper,] what's wrong [with you?]

COOPER. [Don't touch] me!!

(She backs away as **THOMAS** reaches deep into his bag, feeling around for something and comes up with a large towel.)

THOMAS. This will help with the clean up at a reasonable price!

(He sets the towel aside and goes back for more.)

COOPER. It was horrible. The sea creatures.

VANESSA. Ugh, that smell.

COOPER. The tentacled sea creatures.

VANESSA. What about them?

COOPER. In old-fashioned swimwear.

VANESSA. What about them?

COOPER. Under the dock.

VANESSA. Are you serious with this?

COOPER. In old-fashioned swimwear! Under the dock!

VANESSA. Okay, this sentence construction is really frustrating, Cooper. Clearly something awful happened, but I don't know what you're saying.

(**THOMAS** *pulls out a toothbrush and a tube of toothpaste.*)

THOMAS. I think he'll definitely need these!

COOPER. The tentacled sea creatures in old-fashioned swimwear under the dock. They raped me!

(*Pause. Suddenly* **VANESSA** *snaps her fingers in an "ah ha!" moment and points at* **THOMAS**.)

VANESSA. I told you the dock in that woodcut looked familiar!

(*blackout*)

INTERVAL

*(**SQUID** and **OCTOPUS** enter the space. They are still in their swimsuits, but **SQUID** has a top hat. **OCTOPUS** carries the barrel to the center of the stage and prepares an instrument of some kind. In an ideal world, it would be an accordion. But it's probably a guitar that he tunes up and that's just fine. **SQUID** sets up an easel and mounts a piece of poster board with the following message:)*

HELP US SAVE THE PACIFIC NORTHWEST TREE OCTOPUS* The Pacific Northwest tree octopus can be found in the temperate rainforests of the Olympic Peninsula on the Eastern side of the Olympic mountain range, adjacent to Hood Canal. Unlike most other cephalopods, tree octopuses are amphibious, spending only their early life and mating season in an aquatic environment. The rest of the time they freakishly crawl around the trees of the forest.

PLEASE DONATE NOW. Although the tree octopus is not officially listed as an Endangered Species, we feel it should be added since its numbers are critically low for breeding. The reasons for this dire situation include: logging and suburban encroachment; pollution; predation by foreign species such as wicked house cats; and booming populations of its natural predators, including the bald eagle and the sasquatch. Unless immediate action is taken to protect this species and its habitat, the Pacific Northwest tree octopus will be but a memory. You can make a difference for this rare, disturbing species.

*Please note: no portion of the money raised tonight to save the Pacific Northwest Tree Octopus will go to save the Pacific Northwest Tree Octopus. Because they are creepy and wrong.

*(**SQUID** sets the top hat down on the ground and picks up a tambourine. The pair launch into a stripped down, street busker rendition of something like Bonjovi's "Living on a Prayer" or Aerosmith's "Janie's Gut a Gun." It might be one song, but it might be more if everyone's having fun.)*

ACT TWO

(Lights rise on a bare stage except for a single chair. **COOPER** *is in the chair, slumped down. He is wearing "union suit" style long John underwear with a blanket over his shoulders. He has a mug of something warm and soothing. He stares into the cup and perhaps whistles a little tune, but it's a completely dissociative thing.)*

*(***VANESSA*** enters in a rain slicker and carrying a hefty stick of driftwood. She waits. He doesn't look up from the mug.)*

VANESSA. I'm going out now.

COOPER. Mm hm.

VANESSA. To dock.

COOPER. Mm hm.

VANESSA. I said, "I'm going to the dock."

COOPER. This tea is so warm and soothing.

VANESSA. It's chamomile.

COOPER. Yummy.

VANESSA. And I put a lot of gin in it.

*(***COOPER*** looks at the tea and then continues to drink it.)*

COOPER. I understand you've had a traumatic experience. No one hates that more than I do, unexpectedly. It actually hurts my heart if you can believe it. So before I head down to the dock to handle this, and I will handle this, is there anything you want to give me a heads up on? Anything you can tell me to help?

*(***COOPER*** clutches the tea closer and begins to rock a bit.)*

COOPER. What about the dock?

VANESSA. Tell me what exactly happened at the dock?

COOPER. I don't know what you're talking about.

VANESSA. You don't remember anything about what happened at the dock?

COOPER. According to the new and very fragile framework of reality that my brain has urgently created in order to help me remain sane, I'm going to say "no." No, I don't remember anything about the dock.

VANESSA. Well, that's no help.

COOPER. Well, I don't remember anything about the dock.

VANESSA. I'm taking this big stick to beat on the monsters.

COOPER. And I definitely don't remember anything about the monsters.

VANESSA. You said they violated you with giant tentacles.

(**COOPER** *starts screaming. It's more of a constant yelping and yowling in terror. It's hysterical. Then it stops. She waits. He sips his mug of tea & gin.*)

VANESSA. Okay.

COOPER. Wait!

(**COOPER** *is suddenly alert.*)

Who was that man?

VANESSA. What?

COOPER. Who was that man standing here in his underwear with all of the nautically themed tattoos?

VANESSA. He, huh, he wasn't in his underwear.

COOPER. He was. He was in tiny, colorful underwear and you were wrapped up in a sheet.

VANESSA. Wrong.

COOPER. Wrapped in a damp, soiled sheet and being very dramatic.

VANESSA. Dramatic?

COOPER. Very dramatic.

VANESSA. I was no such thing! Your memory of the events is clearly outsized and distorted by your recent and apparently merciless tentacled assault.

(**COOPER** *starts screaming again. And again it's more of a constant yelping and yowling in terror. It's hysterical. Then it abruptly stops. She feels it out…*)

Okay. And that very nice salesman, who generously helped me clean up the gooey mess you spit up on the floor, was modeling a new pair of briefs that I was considering purchasing. For you.

COOPER. Did you buy them for me?

VANESSA. We were interrupted.

COOPER. Right.

VANESSA. By you.

COOPER. Right.

VANESSA. I mean, I would have bought them.

COOPER. That's…nice.

VANESSA. So if you don't have anything to tell me about what happened to you, don't scream, then I'm going to head out. Nothing? Okay then. You know, I've never done anything like this before, but I have to tell you I'm having this really raw protective instinct and I want to exact vengeance for my husband.

COOPER. Nothing happened to your husband.

VANESSA. I'm going to defend your honor.

COOPER. With a big stick.

VANESSA. It's all very exciting.

(*He gives her a hurt look.*)

COOPER. Exciting?

VANESSA. Well, not all of it. But everything from this point forward I mean. That earlier stuff wasn't exciting; it was very, very unfortunate.

COOPER. Luckily I have no idea what you mean by that.

VANESSA. Because you don't remember any of it?

COOPER. Nope.

VANESSA. But you do remember the man in his underwear?

COOPER. You said he wasn't in his underwear.

VANESSA. See, now I think you're having some very selective amnesia.

COOPER. Never heard of it.

VANESSA. Cooper, of course you've heard of selective amnesia.

COOPER. Well if I had heard of it then I probably would know that I wouldn't remember having heard of it.

VANESSA. Ugh, I'm a patient woman, but you're making this really difficult.

COOPER. You're not a patient woman.

VANESSA. Well, I'm doing my very best to resemble a patient woman.

COOPER. Look, just don't go; I don't think it's a good idea.

VANESSA. And I do think it's a good idea.

COOPER. You also thought knitting was a good idea and somehow the cat ended up dead.

VANESSA. We agreed to never talk about that.

COOPER. You agreed we'd never talk about that!

VANESSA. Because it was an accident!

COOPER. I loved that cat!

VANESSA. Don't you say you loved that cat in a tone that makes it sound like I didn't love that cat!

COOPER. We can visit his little kitty seaside grave to see how much you loved that cat. Oh wait, you never go there!

VANESSA. It's too hard!

COOPER. Tell it to kitty!

VANESSA. You bastard. I'm heading out into the face of uncertainty to seek biblical-style vengeance on your behalf. I bathed you while you were in a catatonic state and still smelled like fish guts. While you whimpered in your sleep I searched the beach for a piece of driftwood with just the right heft to really crush some skulls. I put gin in your warm tea unprompted. And this is the thanks I get?

COOPER. Clearly I refuse to remember key events from earlier in the story in order to stay sane, but you're going to do whatever it is you're going to do because you're bored and you're caught up in the excitement of all of this.

VANESSA. That's true!

COOPER. Thank you!

VANESSA. But it's more than that!

COOPER. I think I need more tea.

VANESSA. I think you need some valium.

COOPER. I know I need more gin!

VANESSA. Get it yourself!

COOPER. Maybe I will!!

(VANESSA *takes a deep breath and suddenly transforms, becoming warm and comforting.*)

VANESSA. Honestly, Cooper, seeing you like this. Seeing you so completely destroyed and sexually demoralized, it's really unlocked something deep inside of me. I feel like now, instead of seeing you as the cold, withholding man I thought you were, I can see you as the weak, terrified, and helpless man you are. And that's something I can work with.

COOPER. Fuck you.

VANESSA. I understand your need to lash out.

COOPER. Fuck you again.

VANESSA. It's healthy.

COOPER. You don't understand a damn thing.

VANESSA. No, it is absolutely healthy for you to process these [insecurities.]

COOPER. [And stop] being so fucking kind.

VANESSA. I'm saying awful truths to you, Cooper. I'm being nice, not kind.

COOPER. Whatever you're being, stop it.

VANESSA. You just stay here and rest up.

COOPER. What is happening with this mannered tone you've adopted?

VANESSA. It's called love.

COOPER. It sounds creepy.

VANESSA. Renewed love.

COOPER. You sound creepy.

VANESSA. A love I had almost abandoned.

COOPER. I said, "Stop it!"

VANESSA. I'll take care of everything.

*(She kisses him on the cheek and heads out. **THOMAS** enters again, fully dressed, bag in hand. He pulls the old-fashioned microphone onto stage and a spotlight appears again. He taps the microphone for sound and then clears his throat.)*

THOMAS. There really are just so many wonderful things about living in a seaside town. I can't stress that enough.

(He covers the microphone and leans it to one said.)

In spite of what you might have heard. Stories get so exaggerated as they're told over and over, you wouldn't believe. I mean, just the most awful stories.

(He returns to the microphone.)

But this lovely seaside town does have the natural beauty that I often mention, of course, and the "fisherman's" lifestyle, calloused hands, hard-working ethic, all of that. And living next to the mysteries of the dark waters as they churn away.

(He covers the microphone again.)

Now, to clarify, that bit is really meant to be more of an existential thing, a reflective thing: staring into the murky depths and asking yourself questions about life. It's doesn't mean you should actually investigate the mysteries in the dark waters. That could get you into trouble. For example, the mysteries of the dark water might sexually assault you.

(He returns to the microphone.)

Luckily, you don't have to worry too much in the event that something terribly unfortunate does happen because someone like me is making the rounds with just what you need, both physically and mentally. And I'm happy to deliver anything I can get my hands on. I'm happy to do anything I can to help.

(He sets the microphone aside again as the spotlight fades. He makes sure the cord is out of the way and then knocks in the air as if on a door. He stamps his foot to add the Foley sound. **COOPER** *looks up, startled by the knocking and suspicious.)*

COOPER. Who is it?

THOMAS. Salesman.

COOPER. No, thank you. Go away.

THOMAS. Travelling salesman.

COOPER. I said, "No, thank you. Go away."

*(***THOMAS*** *loosens his tie and unbuttons a few buttons, revealing more tattoo work.)*

THOMAS. Alt-attractive travelling salesman.

COOPER. Why would that information change my answer in any way?

THOMAS. Attractive in an alternative way, you understand.

COOPER. Go away!

THOMAS. I also have a wide array of soothing balms and psychotropic drugs.

COOPER. Well then.

(He gets up and heads to the door. **THOMAS** *strides right past him into the room.)*

Wait, you were here yesterday.

THOMAS. I did pay a call to your home yesterday and "demonstrated" a few items for your lovely wife, but I thought it a good idea to come back today and check in on the man of the house. See how you're feeling? I'm Thomas, Thomas Bell.

COOPER. Cooper Minnow.

THOMAS. Now we've had a proper introduction. It's a pleasure to meet you under happier and less traumatic circumstances, Mr. Minnow.

COOPER. Cooper's fine.

THOMAS. Cooper.

COOPER. And I'm fine, everything's fine; it's just another morning.

THOMAS. Oh good. That's good. I was worried there might be some lingering soreness or psychological damage.

COOPER. I'm sure I don't know what you're talking about.

THOMAS. All right.

COOPER. But if there were, hypothetically, lingering soreness and psychological damage, this is purely conjecture you understand, then what kind of products would you recommend?

THOMAS. Please have a seat.

(**COOPER** *sits down and then hops back up.*)

COOPER. Oh, wait one sec!

(*He rushes off.* **THOMAS** *sets his bag down on the wooden block and opens it. He then takes off his tie and opens his shirt, making himself more comfortable.*)

THOMAS. This is quite a spare little home you have here. It's such an interesting design choice, very bold.

(**COOPER** *returns with a handle of gin.*)

COOPER. No, it's not. It's just empty. Sorry to leave you in here, but I told my wife I'd get this myself and now I have.

THOMAS. That demonstrates that you are still in control of your own choices.

COOPER. Yes. It does.

THOMAS. Now, please relax and I'll make my presentation.

(**COOPER** *drinks the gin straight from the bottle and sits down.*)

COOPER. Shoot.

THOMAS. Here we go. There are so many wonderful things about living in this seaside town: the cool, crisp air, the salty smell that keeps you a little more alert, the lush greenery climbing up from craggy rocks and gray sand, like [unexpected plumes...]

COOPER. [I'm not interested] in any of this.

THOMAS. I'm sorry?

COOPER. This part is very misleading. Based on my recent experiences that I can't remember because I would repeatedly kill myself. If you're trying to sell me on the natural beauty of this place, that's gonna be an [uphill climb.]

THOMAS. [I'll just skip] to the end of this part.

COOPER. Just skip to the balms and drugs.

(*He reaches into his bag and starts pulling out creams and pill bottles. A lot of creams and pill bottles in varied shapes, sizes, and colors. He begins examining them.*)

THOMAS. I have quite a variety. Let's see which ones are right for you.

COOPER. There are so many.

THOMAS. Ah, here, take one of these.

(*He pops a pill from one of the bottles.*)

COOPER. What is it?

THOMAS. It's calming to the nerves.

COOPER. Is it okay to take it with alcohol?

THOMAS. It doesn't say anything about that on the label. It doesn't even have a label, so I'm sure it's fine.

(**COOPER** *takes the pill.* **THOMAS** *is already opening other bottles and pulling out other pills.*)

And this one is for any pain you might be experiencing?

COOPER. Okay.

THOMAS. And this one helps numb the pinch of persistent bad memories.

COOPER. I'll take two of those.

THOMAS. And this one is for that offending "fishy" odor.

COOPER. I don't smell anything.

THOMAS. Trust me.

(**COOPER** *takes the pills and washes them down with gin.*)

COOPER. Easy to swallow.

THOMAS. Now just give that all a few minutes to work it's way into your blood stream and you should be on the mend. Oh and this…

(*He pulls an adorable stuffed puppy out of the bag.*)

You hug this stuffed puppy and it provides emotional comfort.

COOPER. I really don't think so.

THOMAS. You'd be amazed at the way stroking it can be really centering.

(**THOMAS** *holds it out at about waist level and waits.* **COOPER** *reluctantly strokes the puppy. Clearly it makes him happy.*)

You see?

COOPER. Yes, it feels good to stroke it.

THOMAS. You just keep stroking it while those pills kick in.

(**COOPER** *takes the puppy in his arms and hugs it to his chest.*)

COOPER. What about the balms and ointments?

THOMAS. We've got cucumber, vanilla, pomegranate, boysenberry, rough rock salt, don't pick that one, but any of the others. There really are a lot of choices. But you'll want to try those for yourself as you'll no doubt need to apply them in sensitive and private areas.

COOPER. Oh. Okay.

THOMAS. Yes. So, I'll just total this up. I do it all in my head, all of the figures and taxes. So we've got the pills, the puppy, oh, which ointment?

COOPER. Pomegranate.

THOMAS. Pomegranate.

(He begins to do math on his fingers.)

COOPER. What about the underwear?

THOMAS. Excuse me?

COOPER. My wife said she was going to buy some colorful underwear for me yesterday but I interrupted?

THOMAS. Oh, of course! Of course, the underwear. Right.

COOPER. Do you have those?

THOMAS. As it happens, I'm wearing the same sample pair.

COOPER. That's convenient.

THOMAS. Isn't it?

COOPER. But maybe less than hygienic.

THOMAS. I assure you that I take personal hygiene very seriously.

COOPER. That is an admirable quality. So then can I see the underwear?

THOMAS. Oh. Hmmm.

*(***THOMAS*** looks over his shoulder at the door.)*

COOPER. I'm starting to feel a little woozy.

THOMAS. Are you now?

(He begins stripping down to the underwear.)

All right then, yes. Let me just show you these. First you'll notice that the color is just the thing to put the spring back in your step, even if you're the only one that knows you're wearing it.

COOPER. It is bold.

THOMAS. And the stitching really is above par for any undergarments you'll find in town. The fit can also be customized. And the material, well, I can't say enough about the feel of the material against your skin.

COOPER. They do look good.

THOMAS. You should try them on.

(**THOMAS** *begins to take off the underwear.*)

COOPER. Wait! Wait!

(**THOMAS** *stops.*)

THOMAS. You don't want to try them on?

COOPER. While I appreciate your verve and selfless salesmanship, I'm not sure having a naked man in the middle of the living room is exactly what I need right now. Although I am feeling much more relaxed.

THOMAS. I told you those pills were just the thing.

COOPER. And the gin.

THOMAS. And the gin.

COOPER. I'm starting to get warm, is it warm in here?

THOMAS. Feels the same to me.

COOPER. No, it's warmer.

THOMAS. Probably means the shock is wearing off. If you had experienced shock, I mean. And you are wearing those full body long johns. They must trap in your body heat.

COOPER. They do.

THOMAS. That's why you need a pair of briefs like these. Perfect for staying cool and letting the sea air caress the skin.

COOPER. Maybe you're right.

(**THOMAS** *looks over his shoulder again.*)

THOMAS. I completely understand your desire to maintain decorum in your living room. Why don't we step back into the bedroom and you can try these on. With some privacy.

COOPER. You think?

THOMAS. I really do.

COOPER. Well then maybe we should.

THOMAS. After you.

(**COOPER** *heads off, unbuttoning his long underwear.* **THOMAS** *picks through the tubes of lotion, finds one he likes, and takes it with him as he heads after* **COOPER**.)

(**SQUID** *and* **OCTOPUS** *enter again.* **OCTOPUS** *hops up on the barrel and gets comfortable. He has several Band-Aids on his arms and legs.* **SQUID** *leans against the wall with her seashell.*)

OCTOPUS. So I really need some Bactine or something, it [really hurts.]

SQUID. [So I told you not] to mess around with that sea turtle.

OCTOPUS. Um, so that sea turtle was cute.

SQUID. Um, so that sea turtle was old.

OCTOPUS. Ageist.

SQUID. And that rough skin, navigating the shell. So how did [you even...?]

OCTOPUS.

(*mocking her...*)

"[Navigating that] shell." Well that's why I'm all scraped up, isn't it.

SQUID. So there's no need to get bitchy.

(**VANESSA** *enters. With her stick. She is serious.* **SQUID** *and* **OCTOPUS** *give her a deadpan stare.*)

VANESSA. Nice swimsuits.

SQUID & OCTOPUS. Thanks.

VANESSA. Do you two usually hang out under this dock?

SQUID & OCTOPUS. Maybe.

VANESSA. Do you always speak in unison?

SQUID & OCTOPUS. Maybe.

VANESSA. Would you happen to be tentacled sea creatures in disguise?

SQUID & OCTOPUS. Maybe.

VANESSA. What is that, some kind of magical sea creature thing?

SQUID & OCTOPUS. Yep.

VANESSA. Well, I think you met my husband yesterday.

SQUID & OCTOPUS. So…?

VANESSA. He's a fisherman.

SQUID. Oh, so you're Cooper's wife? Wow! Isn't he great? He's so great. And really well equipped, right? I mean, he has an impressive piece of "equipment." That was so much fun, wasn't that so much fun?

OCTOPUS. (*Deadpan.*) So. Much. Fun.

SQUID. I mean, when I say that was an incredible party you'll just have to understand that I couldn't do it justice if I tried. So fun!

OCTOPUS. (*Deadpan.*) So. Much. Fun.

SQUID. And it's so open minded of you as a wife, as a modern woman, to let him play with us like that.

VANESSA. I don't let him "play."

SQUID & OCTOPUS. Oh.

VANESSA. And I'm not sure you can call what you did "play."

SQUID. Well, I'm not sure you were here to know what to call it.

OCTOPUS. You're general countenance isn't very upbeat, is it?

SQUID. Mmm, not at all.

VANESSA. You two raped my husband.

(*They laugh at her.*)

It's not funny!

SQUID & OCTOPUS. Sorry.

VANESSA. I've come here to exact revenge on his behalf.

SQUID. Look, I'm a squid. It was hard enough just to drag myself up on the beach to chill out. If some nice piece of ass is going to present himself to me and I don't have to do any work? Well, that's really a no brainer. And when that juicy morsel is moping, lamenting the wife he loves but feels like he can never ever satisfy?

OCTOPUS. That's clearly you.

SQUID. Its so you. And it's sad.

VANESSA. He, wait, he said that?

SQUID. Awww…he did. So then I felt obligated to generously take his mind of things.

OCTOPUS. And I just wanted to fuck him.

VANESSA. I am going to beat you with this stick.

SQUID. Just to be clear, you see two "people" in swimsuits. So you have absolutely no idea what you're getting into.

VANESSA. I don't care what you really are because no one gets away with hurting that pathetic, ridiculous man. Because he's my pathetic, ridiculous man and I'm about to fuck you up.

SQUID. So you think you can take both of us, huh?

(**OCTOPUS** *starts checking his fingernails. He's not really interested in any of this.*)

OCTOPUS. Oh, so you can grapple or fight her or whatever on your own, I'm not really interested in any of this. I don't find her very interesting.

SQUID. Oh, so you found her husband interesting enough, but not her.

OCTOPUS. That's right.

SQUID. You liked him, but not her.

OCTOPUS. So?

SQUID. Fine, that totally cinches it. I'm so sending Mom a letter.

OCTOPUS. Stop threatening to out me to Mom.

SQUID. I bet she already knows, how could she [not know?]

OCTOPUS. [Its nobody's] business. I'm a grown cephalopod, they're my tentacles and I'll put them [where I want.]

SQUID. [It's for your] own good, so take it [down a notch.]

OCTOPUS. [So don't even try] to put that [on me.]

SQUID. [I'm not] judging you, I'm pushing you to accept yourself. It's not easy [out there…]

OCTOPUS. [Please do explain] to me what that's like, oh wait! I already know because I've fucked or been fucked by half the fish [in the sea.]

VANESSA. [Just shut the] fuck up!

(Pause. SQUID and OCTOPUS glare at her.)

As heart warming as this supportive moment might be to anyone else anywhere ever, I don't care one fucking bit about any of your bizarre family business or issues of self-acceptance.

SQUID & OCTOPUS. So rude.

VANESSA. Let's do this.

SQUID & OCTOPUS. So come and get it.

(SQUID and OCTOPUS back out of sight. VANESSA charges after them brandishing the stick.)

(Suddenly COOPER enters wearing the colorful underwear that THOMAS was selling. He crashes down into the chair, drinking a gigantic glass of water, props his feet up on the wooden block, and wipes the sweat off of his face. THOMAS follows. He is only wearing his pants, still open, or maybe just a towel, and his tattooed upper body is visible. He is also drinking a huge glass of water.)

THOMAS. Hydration is so important.

COOPER. I will buy this underwear.

THOMAS. So glad you're pleased.

COOPER. And that lotion, too. Your "application technique" was, was just, I don't know what to say. I mean, I was feeling sore and tender and timid and raw, but now just…wow.

(THOMAS clinks his water glass against COOPER's.)

I mean you did things I've never done, things I didn't even know to do. But now I do.

THOMAS. Now you do.

COOPER. Whoa.

THOMAS. You don't think your wife will be home anytime soon?

COOPER. Ha! I don't even know what day it is, those pills are something else.

THOMAS. And the gin.

COOPER. And the gin!

THOMAS. But if she did walk in and find us like this, well, that would be the kind of thing that usually happens to me right around now, in these kinds of scenarios I mean, and it's never very pleasant.

COOPER. She has a big stick.

THOMAS. Excuse me?

COOPER. She has a big stick with her. She went somewhere with a big stick. And there was something about violence.

THOMAS. Well, that doesn't sound good.

COOPER. Thomas Bell, can I call you Tom?

THOMAS. I prefer Thomas.

COOPER. That's a shame. "Tom" is so much more approachable. But I will respect your wishes, Thomas, because I'm a respectful kind of guy. And I like to make people happy if I can. I can't ever, but I try. So, Thomas, if my wife wants to carry around a big stick and beat things into submission, then that's fine by me.

THOMAS. Maybe she's just looking for an outlet.

COOPER. I think she might be psychotic.

THOMAS. An outlet for her emotions. She might have pent up feelings that she hasn't been able to express properly, so she's channeling them into a new activity, in this case: unchecked aggression.

COOPER. Right, "psychotic."

THOMAS. Maybe your needs just aren't lining up in a healthy way.

COOPER. That all sounds a bit like wishy washy pop-psychology. That wasn't a nice thing for me to say.

Listen, it's not that I don't want to understand her or connect or any of that; it's just that I've felt so stuck for so long. But then again, after what you just did in there, I'm feeling unstuck and my eyes are suddenly open wider.

THOMAS. You're welcome.

COOPER. Unfortunately I'm just not sure I can salvage this marriage now.

THOMAS. Not with that attitude.

COOPER. It would take some kind of, I don't know, some kind of harrowing moment to bring us back together now. And that kind of thing doesn't happen in real life. Not my life, anyway. I'm just a fisherman.

THOMAS. Okay, I'm hearing you, but that kind of moment can absolutely happen. To anyone. Let me tell you a personal story, something private that has to do with one of my tattoos, to try and contextualize it for you. How's that?

COOPER. Your tattoos?

THOMAS. Each one has a different story. Like little episodes that tell the story of my life.

COOPER. This all seems very familiar. Not "I've done this before" familiar, but "sharing personal details" familiar. You should maybe be on your way, [shouldn't you?]

THOMAS. [Mr. Minnow,] please. I'm not asking for intimacy. I understand that was a new experience for you and you might not be totally comfortable yet, but try to still that knee-jerk reaction, no one's falling in love.

COOPER. Sorry. Of course, of course please go ahead with your personal tattoo story. Is it about that big anchor on your arm?

THOMAS. No. That's just an anchor. It's about this green fish here. Now, just sit back and listen.

(As **THOMAS** *starts to tell his story, the lights in the room dim a bit and gentle underscoring begins as petite foot lights in front of the small puppet theater rise. The* *events of* **THOMAS***' story unfold on the little stage with puppets.* **COOPER** *is delighted.)*

COOPER. Ohhhh.

THOMAS. When I was still a novice traveling salesman, I didn't yet know how to gauge the danger of situations as I moved from house to house.

(Little **THOMAS** *with his little bag passes houses.)*

One day I happened to find myself on a small raft in the sea. All alone. Or so I thought.

(Little **THOMAS** *is on a little raft in the water.)*

COOPER. I don't like this.

THOMAS. As I pondered my predicament, the water near me started to move and dance. Suddenly an immense fish began to rise from the water. It had a gigantic mouth full of razor teeth, [scales like…]

COOPER. [I said,] "I don't like this."

(A little sea monster rises out of the water. And then suddenly, a screeching roar that shakes the house is heard followed by **VANESSA***'s screaming from far away.)*

VANESSA. *(from off)* Cooper!!!

(As **COOPER** *and* **THOMAS** *jump up, the puppet theater goes still, all of the lights abruptly restore and any underscoring vanishes.)*

COOPER. That sounded like Vanessa.

(The screeching roar sounds again. Then closer now…)

VANESSA. *(from off)* Cooper, open the door!!!!

THOMAS. That does sound like [your wife.]

COOPER. [What's she] saying?

(Much closer…)

VANESSA. *(from off)* Cooper, open the fucking door!!!!

THOMAS. What's going on?!

*(***COOPER** *rushes off and then falls back onto the stage in horror.)*

*(The screeching roar is deafening as **VANESSA**, bruised, bloodied, and wet, drags herself on with an enormous tentacle wrapped around her lower leg. It is truly huge and clearly gets larger as it trails offstage. It is trying to pull her back as she claws her way forward, struggling against it.)*

COOPER. Oh my god!

VANESSA. It didn't go as I imagined! They took away my stick. Also, fucking help me!!!

THOMAS. I know I have something to help!

*(As he digs through his bag, he begins pulling out random, insane items: a badminton racquet, a ukulele, an earhorn, a desk lamp, a rotary dial phone, etc. As he does this, **COOPER** rushes over and grabs **VANESSA**'s hand. He pulls.)*

COOPER. I've got you!

VANESSA. Ow!

COOPER. I have a good grip!

VANESSA. You're stretching me [like taffy!]

COOPER. [I won't let] you go!

VANESSA. Do something else!!

*(**COOPER** loses his grip and **VANESSA** tumbles back, rolling, so that the tentacle wraps further up her body.)*

COOPER. No!

THOMAS. Found it!

*(**THOMAS** comes up with the hatchet. The very first thing he pulled out of his bag earlier in the story. **COOPER** grabs the hatchet from **THOMAS** and rushes off past the tentacle.)*

COOPER. Let go of my wife!

*(**COOPER**'s impassioned screaming mixes with the screeching roar and suddenly (**VANESSA** falls onto the stage, pulling the now severed and gory stump of the tentacle into view.)*

(**COOPER** *walks on after it, covered in purple puss and gore, brandishing the hatchet like an action hero. There is a moment of heroic posing in the doorway. He then rushes to* **VANESSA** *and helps her get free of the severed tentacle. They embrace and all at once…*)

COOPER. Are you okay?!

VANESSA. I thought I might die!

COOPER. I thought you might die!

VANESSA. But I didn't, you saved me!

COOPER. You're safe now!

VANESSA. Thank you!

COOPER. I'm so glad [you're all right!]

VANESSA. [Oh, I'm sorry I] couldn't bludgeon them with [vengeance for you.]

COOPER. [No, I'm so sorry that I] was caught up in my own complete nervous breakdown that I [let you go alone.]

VANESSA. [And I'm sorry I called] you a little man; you're not a little man. You're a huge man everywhere [that counts.]

COOPER. [And I'm sorry I] neglected you out of feelings of fear and inadequacy instead of talking to you [and trying to solve it]

VANESSA. [And I'm sorry I made it so] hard to talk to me by mocking and maligning [you day in and day out.]

COOPER. [I'm sorry I forgot all of the] reasons I fell in love with you when I still love you [and I do still love you.]

VANESSA. [And I'm sorry I let our marriage] get stale like I didn't have [any choice when I clearly did.]

COOPER. [And I'm sorry I've been slowly] poisoning you for weeks out of a desperate desire to be free from your [constant haranguing.]

VANESSA. [Is there an] antidote?!

COOPER. Yes!

VANESSA. Then I don't care!

(*They kiss. Passionately.*)

THOMAS. This is so beautiful.

*(They break apart. **VANESSA** looks at **THOMAS** and then **COOPER**.)*

VANESSA. What is he doing here?

COOPER. Helping?

VANESSA. Why is he naked?

COOPER. Ah.

THOMAS. Well, I should be getting dressed now I think. Ill just send you a bill via post, Mr. Minnow.

COOPER. Yes, of course.

THOMAS. If I could just get my hatchet back?

*(He takes the hatchet from **COOPER**.)*

Thank you. And I'll get my things.

COOPER. Yes, of course.

*(**THOMAS** tosses things back in the bag. This may take a while, It might bring everything to a crashing halt and be incredibly awkward for **COOPER** and **VANESSA** as they exchange glances and whisper about how long its taking. Once everything is packed up, **THOMAS**. notices the tentacle.)*

THOMAS. Oh, and if you don't want that, I'll just happily take it.

COOPER. Hurry up.

*(**THOMAS** picks up the end of the tentacle and drags it off with him into the bedroom. **VANESSA** and **COOPER** are alone.)*

VANESSA. He's going to get tentacle juice all over the bedroom.

COOPER. I don't care.

(He kisses her again.)

I love you.

VANESSA. And I love you, too.

COOPER. This harrowing experience has changed me.

VANESSA. It was harrowing, wasn't it?

COOPER. I want us to be better.

VANESSA. And I desperately want that, too!

COOPER. It's terrible that we were both sexually violated by those despicable sea monsters.

VANESSA. Oh.

COOPER. It's awful, but it really puts us on common ground to start over again fresh.

VANESSA. Um.

COOPER. There's no reason to pretend it didn't happen to me now that we have a shared understanding of the [horrors that…]

VANESSA. [No, no, they] didn't rape me.

COOPER. What?

VANESSA. No, no. We brawled and clashed and they took my stick away and there was a lot of smack talk while they tried to crush me to death, but they didn't rape me.

COOPER. Oh.

VANESSA. But I still understand.

COOPER. Okay, sure.

VANESSA. We still have common ground.

COOPER. It's not exactly the same, but I guess.

VANESSA. And we can start fresh.

COOPER. No, no, you're right.

VANESSA. Now, why exactly was Thomas Bell, the alternatively attractive traveling salesman, naked?

COOPER. I can't lie to you, Vanessa. He healed me. He tenderly healed me.

VANESSA. Wait, what?

COOPER. He healed me with pills and soothing balms and physical pleasure.

VANESSA. Oh god.

COOPER. And he showed me things, amazing things I never even knew to do in the bedroom.

VANESSA. Oh god.

COOPER. And now, still riding high on pills, gin, the dizziness of my first same sex experience, and the adrenaline of hacking apart a tentacled sea monster, I'm going to show those things to you.

VANESSA. Really?

(**COOPER** *scoops her up into his arms.*)

COOPER. Really.

VANESSA. Well then we'll throw that stupid, charming salesman out on his ear and you can get down to the business of showing me.

COOPER. Absolutely. I'll start by gently bathing your wounds and then softly kissing every inch of your bruised and battered body. Then I'll drop rose petals all [around your…]

VANESSA. [Cooper, I] just want you to fuck me.

COOPER. Ah.

VANESSA. Just fuck me.

COOPER. That works.

(*He carries her off.*)

(**OCTOPUS** *and* **SQUID** *make their way on.* **OCTOPUS** *climbs on the barrel. One of his arms has a bandaged nub at the end instead of a hand. He is still covered in Band-Aids.* **SQUID** *leans against the wall with her seashell. This time she's listening to it.*)

SQUID. This is so not what the sea sounds like.

OCTOPUS. Who gives a fuck?

SQUID. It's false advertising.

OCTOPUS. He totally cut my hand off!

SQUID. It'll grow back.

OCTOPUS. So what? It still hurts. And not just physically, okay? I mean, after we had such a good time with that fisherman.

SQUID. Truth.

OCTOPUS. I thought that it was maybe something special.

SQUID. You so did not.

OCTOPUS. I so did.

(She laughs at him.)

Don't laugh. I might have loved him.

SQUID. You know, erotomania runs in our family. Mom said so.

OCTOPUS. I don't care because I don't know what that is.

SQUID. It's when you compulsively believe other people are in love with you and that you're in love with them.

OCTOPUS. He did love me.

SQUID. And then he cut off your hand.

OCTOPUS. And then he cut off my hand!

SQUID. So maybe you need some therapy.

OCTOPUS. So maybe we both do.

SQUID. Anyway, it just goes to show you that a good time doesn't always mean they'll call you back.

OCTOPUS. I bet it's because I was trying to crush his sourpuss wife.

SQUID. She was no fun.

OCTOPUS. I so wasn't even going to get involved until she started yelling at us about self-acceptance.

SQUID. Right?

OCTOPUS. She probably ruined something beautiful.

SQUID. Oh my god, get over it.

OCTOPUS. True love.

SQUID. Whatever. She did have a lot of spunk though, so you have to respect that.

OCTOPUS. No, I really don't.

*(**THOMAS BELL** enters carrying his carpetbag. **SQUID** and **OCTOPUS** give him the now familiar deadpan stare.)*

THOMAS. Excuse me. I'm sorry, I was trying to get up onto the dock to buy passage on the next boat, move on to the next town.

SQUID & OCTOPUS. So…?

THOMAS. Ah, well, I seem to have somehow ended up down here instead.

SQUID & OCTOPUS. So…?

THOMAS. Do you happen to know how to get back up there?

SQUID & OCTOPUS. Yes.

THOMAS. Ah. Well, then could you tell me?

SQUID & OCTOPUS. Maybe.

THOMAS. Maybe?

SQUID & OCTOPUS. So that's what we said.

THOMAS. All right.

SQUID. So it all depends on what you give us?

THOMAS. What did you have in mind?

OCTOPUS. Oh, all sorts of things.

SQUID. So what've you got in the bag?

THOMAS. Oh, all sorts of things.

SQUID. Really now?

OCTOPUS. So how hung are you?

THOMAS. Excuse me?

OCTOPUS. Oh, so I asked, "How hung are you?"

THOMAS. You know, I really respect that direct approach.

SQUID & OCTOPUS. So…?

THOMAS. No complaints thus far.

SQUID & OCTOPUS. Good.

(They all smile. Blackout.)